THE TALE OF ALADDIN AND THE WONDERFUL LAMP

A story from the *Arabian Nights*

RETOLD BY ERIC A. KIMMEL

ILLUSTRATED BY JU-HONG CHEN

HOLIDAY HOUSE / NEW YORK

To Doris, who keeps the lamp burning
E.A.K.

For my daughter, Mi-Le
J.-H.C.

Library of Congress Cataloging-in-Publication Data
Kimmel, Eric A.
The Tale of Aladdin and the wonderful lamp : a story from the *Arabian Nights* /
retold by Eric A. Kimmel ; illustrated by Ju-Hong Chen.
p.   cm.
Summary: A retelling of the adventures of Aladdin who,
with the aid of a genie from a magic lamp, fights an evil sorcerer
and wins the hand of a beautiful princess.
ISBN 0-8234-0938-4
[1. Fairy tales.   2. Folklore, Arab.]   I. Chen, Ju-Hong, ill.
II. Aladdin.   III. Title.
PZ8.K527A1   1992   91–814   CIP   AC
398.2—dc20
[E]

AUTHOR'S NOTE

Although "The Tale of Aladdin and the Lamp" is one of the best-known stories in the *Arabian Nights*, some questions exist as to its authenticity. According to Husain Haddawy, the most recent and authoritative translator of the *Nights*, no Arabic text of the story is known to exist prior to the appearance of Antoine Galland's French translation (1704). Galland claimed to have heard the tale in Aleppo, but it is unknown whether his informer, Hanna Diab, wrote the story down. That manuscript is lost, if it ever existed. Years later, in 1787 and 1805, two Arabic versions of Aladdin appeared in Paris, coincidentally. These were subsequently unmasked as forgeries; retranslations of Galland's French version.

Is "Aladdin and the Lamp" an authentic Arabic tale or a French imposter in Oriental garb?

Only the *djinn* know for sure.

ERIC A. KIMMEL
August 15, 1991

Long ago, in a distant city on the borders of China, there lived a clever but lazy youth named Aladdin. His father had died years before, leaving Aladdin's mother to take in washing in order to feed herself and her young son. She had no money to send Aladdin to school, and he refused to help her wash clothes. So while the poor woman struggled with mountains of laundry, Aladdin idled away his time in the bazaar, begging coins and stealing sweets.

One day, as Aladdin sat playing knucklebones with his companions, a tall man in the black robes of an African magician strolled by. Seeing Aladdin, he stopped and stared.

"You, boy! What is your name?"

"I am Aladdin, the son of Abbas the sandalmaker."

The stranger threw his arms around the youth. "You are the one I seek. Dear Aladdin, I am your uncle, your father's long lost brother!"

Aladdin could not think of a word to say. He never knew his father had a brother, or any other relative.

The stranger went on, "And your mother?"

"She is well. We live not far from here."

"Clever boy!" the magician exclaimed. He gave Aladdin a silver dirham. Then he said, "I will come by tonight. Tell your mother to expect me."

True to his word, the magician arrived that evening, carrying a dinner of roast lamb, sweetmeats, and pastries. After the meal, he asked Aladdin which one of the city's many schools he attended.

Aladdin hung his head in shame. He knew no more of schools than a fish knows of dry land.

"Then perhaps you are learning a trade?"

Aladdin's mother broke in. "He follows no trade but that of idler."

"This does our family no honor," Aladdin's uncle said. "Tomorrow I will look for a suitable shop in which to start Aladdin in business as a merchant. It is the least I can do for my dear brother's memory."

Aladdin met his uncle in the bazaar the next morning. Together they passed through the stalls examining goods from distant lands. They stopped to buy Aladdin a new suit of clothes. Then they walked on, discussing many things, until they reached the city gates.

"Uncle, it is time to go back," Aladdin said.

"But a little farther, dear nephew. I have something to show you."

Aladdin followed his uncle to a rocky hillside several miles from the city. The magician waved his hand. Lo and behold, an iron door with a ring in its center appeared before them.

"Take hold of the ring!" Aladdin's uncle commanded. Aladdin hurried to obey. He gave the ring a tug. The iron door swung open to reveal a flight of stairs descending deep into the earth.

"Listen closely. Your life depends on it," Aladdin's uncle told him. "Follow these stairs downward. You will come to a room filled with jars overflowing with gold and silver coins. Take nothing. If you let so much as the hem of your cloak brush the wall, you will die. Beyond this room you will find a cavern filled with trees bearing rich fruit. Again, take nothing. Follow the path through the cavern. At its end you will find an old brass lamp burning in a niche in the wall. Put out the flame, pour out the oil, and bring the lamp back to me. When you return, you may take anything you like, for nothing can harm you as long as you hold the lamp." He removed the ring from his hand and slipped it on Aladdin's finger. "This will protect you from whatever evil may be lurking along the way. Go swiftly."

Aladdin descended the stairs. He found everything as his uncle described it: the overflowing jars; the trees laden with lustrous fruit. In the wall at the end of the path he found a niche which held an antique lamp. "A poor reward for such trouble," Aladdin thought. He blew out the flame, poured out the oil, tucked the lamp inside his shirt, and hurried back the way he had come. As he passed through the cavern, he filled his pockets with fruit from the trees and coins from the jars. Then he started up the stairs.

Before he reached the top he heard his uncle's voice. "Hurry, Aladdin. Hand me the lamp!"

"Why so impatient, Uncle? It is but an old lamp, is it not?"

"That is none of your business."

"Then I will make it so. Tell me why this lamp is important. Otherwise I will keep it."

"Keep it then, for all the good it will bring you!" The magician waved his hand once more. The iron door disappeared in a flash of light, trapping Aladdin underground.

Three days and nights passed while Aladdin lay huddled in the darkness below ground. Tormented by hunger and thirst, he attempted to eat the fruits in his pockets. He found them hard as glass. The coins were equally useless. Aladdin threw them away. In despair he clasped his hands together. In doing so he rubbed the ring. A burst of light filled the cavern and a *djinn* appeared. Aladdin looked up in terror, but the *djinn*, bowing low, said,

"I am the slave of the ring. Command me, O my master."

"Tell me why my uncle has abandoned me?"

"He is not your uncle," the *djinn* said. "He is a wicked magician. By reading the stars, he learned of this cavern. You are the only one who can enter it and live. He intended to leave you here from the first, after he had obtained what he wanted. But I can free you."

"Do so!"

The *djinn* vanished in another burst of light. When Aladdin opened his eyes he found himself standing in an open field. Moonlight shone down on his face. Never had the night air smelled so sweet.

Aladdin hurried back to the city. When he reached home his mother threw her arms around him, for she had given him up for dead. She laughed when he told her of his strange adventure underground. Only when he showed her the glassy fruits did she believe him. "Is there nothing to eat, Mother?" Aladdin said. "I have not tasted food or drink in three days."

Aladdin's mother shook her head. "Alas, there is no food in the house, nor money to buy any."

Aladdin regretted the coins he had thrown away underground. He did not think of using the ring. But he remembered the lamp. "I will take this relic to the bazaar and sell it. It should bring a few dirhams." He rubbed the lamp with a bit of cloth to polish it. At once a second *djinn* appeared, more terrifying than the first.

The *djinn* bowed low. "I am the slave of the lamp. Command me, O my master."

Aladdin's mother fainted dead away. Aladdin faced the *djinn*. "Can you bring us something to eat?" he stammered, fearful that such a trivial request would offend the mighty *djinn*.

The *djinn* vanished, only to reappear a moment later, bearing a sumptuous feast on silver bowls and platters. Aladdin and his mother ate their fill. The next day Aladdin took the platters to the bazaar and sold them for a good deal of money. There he learned that the lustrous fruits he had found in the underground cavern were not glass at all but precious gems.

On his way home he heard a fanfare of trumpets.

"Make way for Princess Shadjarr ad-Darr! Make way for the Sultan's daughter!"

As the procession passed the spot where Aladdin stood, the curtain of the princess's litter accidentally opened. For one glorious moment Aladdin found himself staring into the loveliest pair of eyes he had ever seen. Almost immediately, someone pulled the curtain shut. The litter passed out of sight. Even so, the deed was done. Aladdin had fallen madly in love. He raced home to tell his mother.

"Mother, I have found the one I wish to marry."

"It pleases my heart. Is she of good family?"

"The best. She is the sultan's daughter, Princess Shadjarr ad-Darr."

Aladdin's mother ran to the door. "Help! Come quickly! My son has gone mad!"

"I am not mad, Mother," Aladdin cried. He poured the jewels he brought from underground into a silver bowl. "Take this bowl to the sultan. Tell him I want to marry his daughter."

Aladdin's mother reluctantly carried the bowl to the palace. Kneeling before the sultan, she cried, "Have mercy, O Mighty Sultan. My son Aladdin, son of Abbas, has lost his wits. He wishes to marry your daughter. He sent me to bring you these trinkets as a token of friendship."

The sultan's eyes gleamed as he examined the gems. His vast treasury contained nothing to equal them. Each stone was worth a kingdom. Composing himself, the sultan said,

"I thank your son for his gift. However, before my daughter can accept him as her bridegroom, he must provide a worthy wedding present. Tell him to bring me forty gold washbasins filled with gems such as these carried by forty strong slaves escorted by forty horsemen mounted on forty chargers."

Aladdin's mother hurried home to tell her son of the sultan's demand. "Your folly will bring us disaster!" she warned.

But Aladdin yawned. "Is that all he wants?"

He took the lamp down from the shelf and rubbed it. "Bring me forty horsemen on forty chargers escorting forty slaves carrying forty gold basins filled with gems," he said when the *djinn* appeared. The *djinn* vanished, but returned in a moment, bringing all the things that Aladdin had requested, as well as a robe of rare silk and a magnificent stallion.

Attired like a prince, Aladdin led his procession of horsemen and slaves to the sultan's palace.

The sultan gasped at such splendor. "Aladdin, son of Abbas, I welcome you as my daughter's bridegroom."

Aladdin bowed low. "Mighty Sultan, grant me one request. Allow me to build a palace worthy of your daughter."

"Certainly, if it pleases you. And when might this palace be finished?"

"By morning."

The Sultan rolled his eyes. Aladdin, the son of Abbas, was either the greatest prince on earth or else completely mad.

That night Aladdin summoned the *djinn*. "Build me a palace whose like was never seen."

A majestic palace arose overnight. Its marble walls sparkled with jewels. Exquisite fountains splashed in its courtyards. Peacocks roamed its fragrant gardens. The sultan could not conceal his astonishment, nor Princess Shadjarr ad-Darr her joy. She and Aladdin were married that afternoon. The celebrations lasted forty days.

Some months later the African magician returned to the city. The moment he heard the tale of the sandalmaker's son who became a prince and built a palace in one night, he immediately grew suspicious. Disguising himself as a peddler of lamps, he walked through the streets crying, "New lamps for old! New lamps for old!"

Princess Shadjarr ad-Darr heard him from her balcony. She remembered Aladdin's old brass lamp. It gave little light, and did not appear to be good for anything. The princess ordered her servants to fetch it. She threw it down to the peddler. "What will you give me for this?"

"More than you can imagine," the magician whispered. He rubbed the lamp. The *djinn* appeared. "Carry this palace and all within it far away to the African desert," the magician commanded. It was done in an instant.

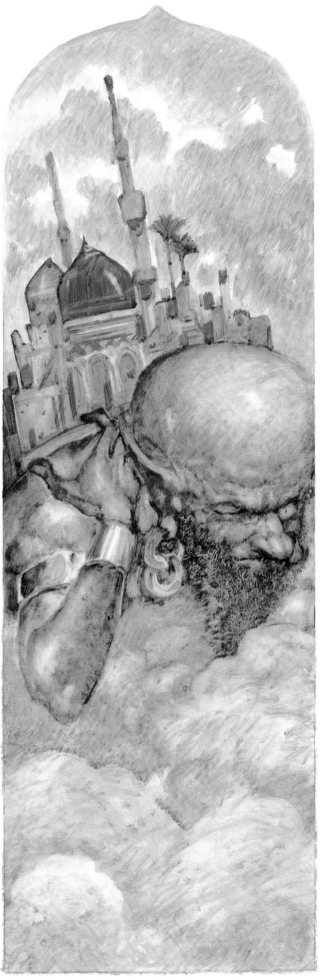

Aladdin and the sultan had gone hunting that day. When they returned in the afternoon, they found an open field where the palace had been. Aladdin stood speechless. Not so the sultan. "Sorcerer! Return my daughter!" His guards seized Aladdin and threw him into the dungeon.

Chained hand and foot, Aladdin languished in darkness. Then he remembered the magic ring. He rubbed it. The *djinn* appeared in a flash of light.

"I am the slave of the ring. Command me, O my master."

"Return Princess Shadjarr ad-Darr to this place."

"I cannot. The *djinn* of the lamp has taken her. He is more powerful than I. But I can bring you to her."

"Do so!"

In an instant Aladdin found himself standing on the burning sands of the African desert. The marble palace's glittering walls rose before him. Aladdin walked through the open gate. He found Princess Shadjarr ad-Darr weeping in the courtyard.

"Do not weep, beloved. I have come to rescue you."

Princess Shadjarr ad-Darr trembled with joy to see him. "Aladdin, I must warn you of the magician . . ."

"I know all about him. We must get back the lamp. Do you know where he keeps it?"

"Underneath his robe. It never leaves his side. But I think I know a way to get it from him."

She told Aladdin her plan.

That night, when the magician returned, Princess Shadjarr ad-Darr asked him to dine with her.

"Why should we quarrel?" she said, smiling, as she filled his cup with wine. "You are a clever man, and very handsome. Can we not be friends?"

The magician sighed with pleasure. As soon as he drained his cup, the princess filled it again. Cup after cup of sweet red wine slipped down his throat. Soon his eyes closed. His robe fell open. Princess Shadjarr ad-Darr slipped the lamp from his side and rubbed it. "Return this palace and all within to where it was before," she commanded when the *djinn* appeared. "But leave that wretch here." She pointed to the magician. Her wish was instantly granted.

The whole city rejoiced at Princess Shadjarr ad-Darr's return. The sultan made amends for putting Aladdin in chains by granting him half his kingdom.

No one ever saw the African magician again. Perhaps he lived; perhaps he died in the desert. Only the *djinn* know for sure.

But as for Aladdin and Princess Shadjarr ad-Darr, they never parted with lamp or ring again, and filled their lives with love and devotion to the end of their days.